Billie B. Brown

www.BillieBBrownBooks.com

Billie B. Brown Books

The Bad Butterfly
The Soccer Star
The Midnight Feast
The Second-best Friend
The Extra-special Helper
The Beautiful Haircut
The Big Sister
The Spotty Vacation
The Birthday Mix-up
The Secret Message
The Little Lie
The Best Project
The Deep End
The Copycat Kid
The Night Fright

First American Edition 2012
Kane Miller, A Division of EDC Publishing

Text copyright © 2010 Sally Rippin
Illustrations copyright © 2010 Aki Fukuoka
Logo and design copyright © 2010 Hardie Grant Egmont

First published in Australia in 2010 by Hardie Grant Egmont

For information contact:
Kane Miller, A Division of EDC Publishing
P.O. Box 470663
Tulsa, OK 74147-0663
www.kanemiller.com
www.edcpub.com
www.usbornebooksandmore.com

Library of Congress Control Number: 2011935665

Printed and bound in the United States of America
5 6 7 8 9 10
ISBN: 978-1-61067-095-1

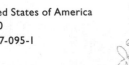

The Bad
Butterfly

By Sally Rippin

Illustrated by Aki Fukuoka

Kane Miller
A DIVISION OF EDC PUBLISHING

Chapter One

Billie B. Brown has two messy pigtails, two pink ballet slippers and one new tutu. Do you know what the "B" in Billie B. Brown stands for?

You guessed it!

Ballerina.

Today Billie has decided that she is going to be a famous ballerina. That is why she is wearing a tutu.

Do you think she looks nice in her new tutu?

Two messy
Pigtails

Tutu

Ballet slippers

3

Billie's best friend is Jack.

Billie and Jack live next door to each other. They do everything together. If Billie decides to play soccer, then Jack will play soccer too. If Jack decides to listen to music, then Billie will too.

If Billie decides to make a super-dooper sandwich with banana and honey and sprinkles, Jack will make a sandwich too. But he prefers salami.

Today Billie and Jack are going to ballet class. What's that? You didn't think boys could do ballet?

Of course they can.

Boys can be very good
ballet dancers.

Billie is wearing her new tutu. Jack is wearing his soccer shorts.

Billie and Jack's new ballet teacher is called Miss Dainty. Billie thinks Miss Dainty is beautiful.

Miss Dainty puts all the girls into one group.

In the group there is a girl called Lola. She is also in Billie's class at school.

Lola's tutu has sparkles on it, and Billie feels a teensy bit **jealous**. Billie wishes she had a tutu with sparkles!

"All right, girls!" says Miss Dainty.

Lola

Billie

"You are all going to
be butterflies. When I
play the piano I want
you to float around
the room like beautiful,
delicate butterflies."

Lola flutters her
arms up and down.
She looks a lot like a
delicate butterfly.

"Lovely, Lola!" says Miss
Dainty.

Billie wants to show
Miss Dainty that she can
flutter her arms like a
butterfly too.

She flaps her arms up and down very fast and spins around.

"**OW!**" says the girl next to Billie. "My toe!"

"**OW!**" says the girl in front of Billie. "My nose!"

"**Watch out!**" says the girl behind Billie. "My glasses!"

"Thank you, Billie,"
Miss Dainty says. "Let's
wait until we are all
ready, shall we?"

Miss Dainty walks over
to the group of boys.
There are only three
boys, including Jack.
Jack waves to Billie.
Billie waves back.

"All right, boys," Miss Dainty says. "I want you to be fierce, stomping trolls. You are fierce, stomping trolls that are trying to catch the dainty butterflies.  Is everyone ready?"

"Yes!" shouts everyone in the class.

Billie shouts the loudest of all. Billie wants to make sure that Miss Dainty knows that she really, really wants to be a beautiful ballerina butterfly.

Chapter Two

"OK, class. Let's get started," Miss Dainty says.

She sits down at the piano. With her right hand she plays a tinkly butterfly tune.

With her left hand she plays a deep, stomping troll tune.

Billie races around the room, flapping her arms. She is a very fast butterfly. Sometimes she accidentally bumps into the other butterflies that get in her way.

"**OW!**" cries one butterfly.

"**Watch it!**" cries another

butterfly.
But Billie
doesn't stop.
She is
a beautiful
ballerina
butterfly,
flying in the breeze.

Jack is a troll. He tries to catch Billie, but she is too fast. Billie is faster than all the butterflies. She is faster than all the trolls! She flaps her arms up and down and runs around the room.

As Billie runs, she looks to see if Miss Dainty is watching.

She wants Miss Dainty to see what a good butterfly she is. But then – **Crash!**

Billie runs straight into the mirror!

"Oh dear!" says Miss Dainty. She rushes over. "I think you'd better slow down, Billie! Are you all right?"

Billie has banged her head. It hurts a lot, but Billie doesn't want to cry in front of Miss Dainty. She sits down and rubs her head and scrunches up her eyes until the **wobbly** feeling goes away.

Miss Dainty puts her cool hand on Billie's forehead. It makes Billie feel much better.

"I'm fine," says Billie in a squeaky voice. "Look!" She flaps her arms up and down like a butterfly with a broken wing.

"All the same, I think you should sit out for a bit and rest," Miss Dainty says.

"I'll stay with her," says Jack.

"Thank you, Jack," says Miss Dainty.

Then she stands up and claps her hands loudly.

Everyone turns around.

"OK, class, let's see
those wings fluttering.
Beautiful, Lola! Yes, that's
right! Come along, trolls.
Let's see your stomping.
Great work!"

Billie hangs her head.
"I'm no good at ballet!"
she says to Jack.

She frowns
and stares at
the ground.

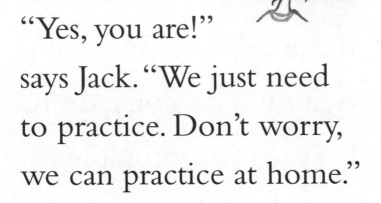

"Yes, you are!"
says Jack. "We just need
to practice. Don't worry,
we can practice at home."

"Really?" says Billie.
"Thanks, Jack."

Chapter Three

That evening, Billie eats her dinner quickly.

"Can I go to Jack's?" she asks her mom and dad.

"No dessert?" asks her dad.

"It's banana pudding!" says her mom.

"I'll have some later," says Billie. "I have to practice my ballet!"

Billie rushes out the back door into the backyard.

In Billie's backyard there is an old wooden fence with a hole in it.

It is just the right size
for Billie and Jack to fit
through!

Billie squeezes through the
hole into Jack's backyard.

Billie looks through Jack's window. She sees that Jack and his family are still eating their dinner.

When Jack sees Billie, he waves and begins to eat very quickly. Jack's dad turns around and waves for Billie to come inside.

"Hi, Billie!" Jack's dad says.

"Jack was just telling me what good dancers you are."

Billie feels very **proud**. She smiles at Jack. "Yes. We're going to be famous ballerinas!" says Billie. "But I still need to practice a bit."

"Let's go!" says Jack, hopping up.

"No dessert?" asks
Jack's mom.

"It's cheesecake!" says
Jack's dad.

"Later!" Billie and Jack
shout together. They run
up to Jack's bedroom.

Billie practices being
a butterfly. Jack practices
being a troll.

Billie flaps her hands fast and flutters around the room. **Crash!**

She bumps into Jack's Lego table. Lego pieces fly everywhere.

Bang! She bumps into Jack's desk. All his Star Wars figures fall on the floor.

"Billie! You are going too fast!" Jack says. "You have to float like a butterfly. Gentle and slow. Like this."

Jack stands on his toes and flaps his arms gracefully.

Then he flutters around the room. Just like a real butterfly.

Billie frowns. She stamps her foot.

"I can't do it," she says. "It's too hard! I'll never be a famous ballerina!"

"You look more like a stomping troll," Jack laughs.

Billie smiles at that.

"Hey," she says. "I've got an idea!"

Chapter Four

All week, Billie and Jack
work on their ballet
after school. Sometimes
they dance in Billie's
bedroom. Sometimes they
dance in Jack's bedroom.

Sometimes their parents
hear them practicing:
Stomp! Stomp! Stomp!

"Are you sure that's
ballet you're doing?"
they call out, when the
stomping gets very loud.

"Yes!" call Billie and
Jack together. "Don't
come in!"

When it's time for their
next ballet class, Billie
and Jack are ready.

Billie puts on her tutu.
Then, instead of her
soft pink ballet slippers,
Billie puts on her big
red boots.

Can you guess what
Billie is up to?

Billie's mom drives Billie
and Jack to dance class.
When they get inside the
hall, Miss Dainty claps
her hands.

"Hello, children," calls
Miss Dainty. "It's very
nice to see you again.

Are you all ready to dance like butterflies and trolls?"

Billie and Jack look at each other and nod.

"Now, Billie, perhaps you can follow Lola today? Jack, you can go over with the boys."

"Um, actually, we've decided to swap parts," Billie says.

"What do you mean?"
Miss Dainty asks.

"Well, Jack is a much
better butterfly than me,"
Billie explains.

"And I think I am a very good stomping troll!"

Miss Dainty smiles. "What a marvelous idea!" she says. "Of course you can be a stomping troll, Billie. And Jack, if you would like to be a butterfly, that's fine with me."

"Yay!" say Billie and Jack together.

Jack flutters around the room, and Billie stomps after him. Jack makes a very good floating butterfly, and Billie makes an excellent troll. They both have lots of fun.

At the end of the lesson, Jack's dad is waiting for them at the front door.

"Well," he says, "how did dance class go tonight? Still going to be a famous ballerina, Billie?"

"Maybe," says Billie, smiling at Jack. "But I think I prefer soccer."